A COMPREHENSIVE GUIDE TO LITERARY THEORIES:CLASSICAL TO CONTEMPORARY

MS DHANYA R, MS. G. SHARMILA DEVI

This book is dedicated to all those who engage passionately with literature—students striving for clarity, teachers nurturing curiosity, and scholars pursuing deeper truths. Your commitment to critical thought and interpretive insight inspires the very purpose of this work. May this volume serve as a companion in your academic journey and encourage continued exploration of the rich and evolving world of literary theory.

Contents

FOREWORD

Literary theory is an essential tool for understanding how texts speak to us and to their times. This book offers a clear and accessible journey through major theoretical frameworks—from Classical thought to Postmodernism—making it an ideal guide for students, educators, and exam aspirants alike. With its structured approach and lucid explanations, it serves not just as a reference but as an invitation to deeper critical inquiry. It is a timely resource for anyone seeking to engage meaningfully with literature and its many interpretations.

Preface

In an era where literary studies continue to evolve rapidly, understanding foundational and contemporary literary theories is essential for scholars, teachers, and students alike. This book offers a clear, concise, yet comprehensive exploration of literary theories — from Classical antiquity to Postmodern innovations — tailored especially for competitive examinations and academic studies.Each chapter is crafted to introduce key thinkers, major ideas, and critical concepts with clarity and scholarly insight. It is my hope that this volume will serve not only as a reference guide but also as a stepping-stone toward deeper inquiry.

Acknowledgements

I would like to express my heartfelt gratitude to all those who have supported me in the completion of this book. My sincere thanks go to my mentors and teachers, whose guidance and scholarly example laid the foundation for my understanding of literary theory. I am equally indebted to my colleagues and peers for their thoughtful discussions and encouragement, which have enriched the scope and clarity of this work. Finally, I wish to acknowledge the contributions of everyone—editors, reviewers, and well-wishers—whose insights and assistance, whether direct or indirect, have helped bring this volume to life.

Prologue

The study of literature is, at its core, a study of human thought, culture, and expression. Over the centuries, literary theory has provided the tools to interpret, question, and reimagine texts in ways that reflect the evolving concerns of society. From the philosophical inquiries of Classical antiquity to the complex critiques of Postmodernism, each theoretical approach offers a unique lens through which literature can be understood.This book is born out of a desire to make these critical frameworks accessible to a wide audience—students preparing for competitive examinations, scholars seeking a clear reference, and anyone curious about the ideas that shape our reading of texts. It is not meant to be exhaustive, but rather foundational: a stepping-stone toward deeper inquiry and critical engagement.In the pages that follow, readers will find concise chapters introducing key thinkers, concepts, and movements in literary theory. My hope is that this volume not only informs but also invites further exploration into the dynamic world of literary criticism.

I

Chapter 1: Classical Literary Theory

Overview:
Classical literary theory was born in ancient Greece and Rome, where philosophers and critics sought to understand the purpose, method, and effect of literature. Their ideas formed the foundation for centuries of critical thought.

Major Thinkers:

- **Plato**
- **Aristotle**
- **Horace**
- **Longinus**

Key Concepts:

- **Mimesis**: Literature as imitation of life or reality (Plato, Aristotle)
- **Catharsis**: Emotional purification or cleansing through art (Aristotle)
- **Decorum**: Appropriateness of style to subject (Horace)
- **Sublimity**: Greatness or loftiness in literary expression (Longinus)

Mimesis (Plato, Aristotle)

- **Meaning:**
  Mimesis means "imitation" in Greek. In the context of literature and art, it refers to the idea that art imitates life, nature, or reality.

- **Plato'sView:**
  Plato was somewhat skeptical of mimesis. In his work *The Republic*, he argued that all art is an imitation of an imitation. Reality, according to Plato, consists of ideal "Forms" (perfect, abstract versions of things). What we see in the physical world is already an imperfect copy of these Forms. Therefore, art — being a copy of the physical world — is two steps removed from true reality. He worried that art could mislead people by appealing to emotions rather than reason.

- **Aristotle'sView:**
  Aristotle, however, had a more positive view in *Poetics*. For him, mimesis is natural to humans and important for learning. He believed that through imitation, artists capture the universal truths about human experience — not just copying reality but re-presenting it in a way that reveals deeper truths.

- Tragedy, for example, imitates serious actions and thus elicits important emotions like pity and fear.

Catharsis (Aristotle)

Meaning:
Catharsis refers to the emotional cleansing or purification that an audience experiences through their engagement with art, especially tragedy.

- **Aristotle'sIdea:**
  In *Poetics*, Aristotle explains that tragedy should arouse pity (*eleos*) and fear (*phobos*) and then purge these emotions. This emotional release benefits the audience psychologically, bringing about renewal and restoration. The tragic events and suffering of characters provide a safe space for spectators to confront deep, often unsettling emotions, leading to a sense of emotional balance and moral clarity afterward.

Decorum (Horace)

- **Meaning:**
  Decorum involves the appropriateness of style to subject matter, audience, and genre.
- **Horace'sIdea:**
  In his *Ars Poetica* (The Art of Poetry), Horace emphasized that different genres and situations require different styles. For instance, a tragic play should use elevated, serious language, while a comedic play can use more colloquial and light-hearted speech. Characters, too, should speak and behave in ways appropriate to their age, social status, and personality. A king should not speak like a servant, and an old man should not act like a reckless youth. Decorum ensures consistency and credibility in a work of art.

Sublimity (Longinus)

- **Meaning:**
  Sublimity refers to a kind of greatness or grandeur in literature that elevates the reader's soul and leaves a lasting impression.
- **Longinus'sIdeas:**
  In *On the Sublime*, Longinus explores what makes certain literary works powerful and unforgettable. Sublimity, he says, transports the reader, producing awe and wonder. It's not just about technical skill but about the greatness of thought, passion, noble diction, and grandeur in style. Sublime writing strikes a balance between the natural greatness of ideas and the mastery of expression, moving beyond the ordinary and stirring deep emotions and admiration.

Main Contributions:

- **Plato** (c. 428–348 BCE)

  - In *The Republic*, Plato criticizes poetry for being a mere imitation of the real world — a "copy of a copy," and therefore dangerous because it appeals to emotions rather than reason.He proposed censoring poets in his ideal state.

- **Aristotle** (384–322 BCE)

  - *Poetics* is the first systematic work of literary theory.

- Defined **tragedy** as "an imitation of an action that is serious, complete, and of a certain magnitude," aiming to evoke **pity and fear** and thereby achieve **catharsis**.

- Introduced the idea of **plot (mythos)**, **character (ethos)**, and **thought (dianoia)** as crucial elements.

- **Horace** (65–8 BCE)

- In *Ars Poetica*, Horace emphasized the importance of **pleasure and instruction** in poetry.
- Advocated for **decorum**: characters must act according to their social class and situation.

- **Longinus** (1st century CE)

- In *On the Sublime*, Longinus explored the concept of **sublimity** in literature — how greatness in writing can transport readers beyond themselves.
- Stressed the role of **inspired passion** and **noble ideas** in achieving sublimity.

II
Chapter 2: Neoclassical Literary Theory

Overview:
In the 17th and 18th centuries, European critics, especially in England and France, revived classical ideals of order, reason, and decorum. Neoclassicism celebrated discipline and formalism.

Major Thinkers:

- **John Dryden**
- **Alexander Pope**
- **Samuel Johnson**

Key Concepts:

- **Order and Balance**
- **Imitation of Nature**

Order and Balance

Meaning:
Order and balance refer to the structured, harmonious arrangement of parts within a work of art or literature. Each element should contribute to a unified whole, with nothing excessive or missing. This reflects a classical ideal where beauty and truth are closely linked to proportion, clarity, and control.

Classical Tradition:

- In ancient Greece and Rome, thinkers like Aristotle and Horace believed that art should avoid extremes. Excessive emotion, chaotic structure, or disproportionate parts would ruin the unity and beauty of a work.
- In literature, this principle is seen in carefully organized plots, well-rounded characters, and measured, appropriate language.
- **Example:** In classical tragedy, the plot follows a clear beginning, middle, and end, without digressions or contradictions.

Importance:
Order and balance allow a work to be both pleasing and instructive. They ensure thatthe reader or viewer is not overwhelmed or confused, but instead guided toward reflection and understanding.

Imitation of Nature

Meaning:

Imitation of nature means that art should reflect the patterns, actions, and experiences found in the real world, particularly those that are universal and true to human life.

Classical Tradition:

- For Aristotle in *Poetics*, literature does not copy nature mechanically but captures its essence, presenting it in a way that reveals underlying truths about human existence.
- Nature, in this view, includes not only the physical world but also human emotions, behaviors, and interactions.
- Good imitation refines and elevates reality. It selects and organizes aspects of life to highlight what is meaningful, rather than merely reproducing random details.

Importance:

Imitating nature helps art to be recognizable and relatable. It creates emotional and intellectual connections between the work and the audience, making the message more powerful and the experience more profound.

Main Contributions:

- **John Dryden** (1631–1700)

    ○ In *An Essay of Dramatic Poesy*, Dryden defends drama as a legitimate literary form.
    ○ Believes drama should mirror nature, but artfully, within classical rules.

- **Alexander Pope** (1688–1744)

    ○ In *An Essay on Criticism*, Pope offers aphorisms about the necessity of rules and the dangers of pride and ignorance in criticism.
    ○ Famous lines: "To err is human, to forgive divine."

- **Samuel Johnson** (1709–1784)

    ○ In *Preface to Shakespeare*, Johnson praised Shakespeare's universality but criticized his neglect of moral instruction and decorum.
    ○ Believed literature should both entertain and morally instruct.

III
Chapter 3: Romantic Literary Theory

Overview:
Romanticism (late 18th to mid-19th century) reacted against Neoclassicism, emphasizing emotion, imagination, and the individual experience.

Major Thinkers:

- **William Wordsworth**
- **Samuel Taylor Coleridge**
- **Percy Bysshe Shelley**

Key Concepts:

- **Imagination over Reason**
- **Emotion over Rationalism**
- **Nature and the Sublime**

Imagination over Reason

Meaning:
In Romanticism, imagination was seen as a higher, more powerful faculty than reason. It was the source of creativity, innovation, and deeper understanding of the world beyond mere logic.

Romantic View:

- Rationalism (logic, science, structured thinking) was seen as limiting.
- Imagination allowed people to see truths hidden from cold analysis — emotional, spiritual, and transcendental truths.
- Poets like **William Blake**, **Samuel Taylor Coleridge**, and **Percy Shelley** believed imagination could "re-create" reality in more meaningful forms, connecting human beings to the infinite and the divine.

Importance:
Imagination enabled artists to explore inner worlds, dreams, myths, and emotions — offering deeper insights into human nature and existence than reason alone could provide.

Emotion over Rationalism

Meaning:

Romantics believed that feelings and intuition were more authentic and valuable guides to truth than strict logic or intellectual analysis.

Romantic View:

- Human beings were seen as emotional and passionate, not simply rational.

- Emotions such as awe, love, sorrow, terror, and joy were central to human life and thus should also be central to art and literature.
- Writers like **Jean-Jacques Rousseau** emphasized the "natural goodness" of feeling over the "corruption" of cold reason.

Importance:

By highlighting emotion, Romantics challenged the idea that reason could solve all problems. They saw feeling as the path to individual freedom, genuine moral understanding, and artistic beauty.

Nature and the Sublime

Meaning:

Nature was revered not just as a backdrop for human activity but as a living, almost spiritual force. The **sublime** refers to experiences of overwhelming beauty, terror, or vastness that transcend ordinary understanding.

Romantic View:

- Nature was seen as a reflection of the divine and a source of inspiration, healing, and truth.
- Experiencing nature could provoke awe and wonder — feelings that took people beyond themselves and pointed toward the infinite (this is the experience of the *sublime*).
- Writers like **William Wordsworth**, **John Keats**, and **Lord Byron** celebrated nature's power and mystery.

Sublime Experiences:

- Standing before vast mountains, stormy seas, or dark forests could create a mix of fear and awe — making people feel both small and connected to something greater.**Edmund Burke** (in *A Philosophical Enquiry into the Origin of Our Ideas of the Sublime and Beautiful*) described the sublime as that which inspires terror and admiration at the same time.

Importance:

Nature and the sublime encouraged spiritual reflection, artistic creation, and a sense of humanity's place within a larger, more mysterious universe.

Main Contributions:

- **William Wordsworth** (1770–1850)

  - In *Preface to Lyrical Ballads*, Wordsworth defines poetry as "the spontaneous overflow of powerful feelings" recollected in tranquility.
  - Advocated for the use of common language in poetry.

- **Samuel Taylor Coleridge** (1772–1834)

  - In *Biographia Literaria*, Coleridge distinguishes between **primary imagination** (the creative power of the mind) and **secondary imagination** (the conscious act of artistic creation).

- **Percy Bysshe Shelley** (1792–1822)

  - In *A Defence of Poetry*, Shelley argued that poets are "the unacknowledged legislators of the world," suggesting poetry shapes human consciousness.

IV

Chapter 4: Victorian Literary Theory

Overview:
The Victorian period (mid to late 19th century) was marked by a tension between art and morality. Critics debated whether literature should uphold social values or exist independently.

Major Thinkers:

· **Matthew Arnold**
· **John Ruskin**
· **Walter Pater**

Key Concepts:

· **Moral Function of Art**
· **Art for Art's Sake**
· **Cultural Criticism**

Moral Function of Art

Meaning:
The *moral function of art* is the idea that art should promote ethical values, teach lessons, and help improve the moral character of its audience.

Viewpoint:

· This idea has ancient roots, going back to **Plato** and **Aristotle**, and was emphasized again in the 19th century by writers like **Matthew Arnold**.
· Art was seen not only as entertainment or aesthetic pleasure but as a means to shape society for the better by reinforcing virtues like compassion, justice, courage, and wisdom.
· Literature, painting, and theatre were expected to inspire moral reflection and provide examples of good and evil, guiding audiences toward virtuous behavior.

Example:

· Victorian novels by writers like **Charles Dickens** (e.g., *Oliver Twist*) often carried strong moral messages about poverty, injustice, and charity.
· Tragedies like **Sophocles' "Antigone"** explore conflicts between personal loyalty and public duty, pushing audiences to reflect on moral choices.

Importance:

Art becomes a tool for social progress and personal growth, helping societies refine their values and strengthen ethical life.

Art for Art's Sake

Meaning:

The slogan *"Art for Art's Sake"* (French: *L'art pour l'art*) means that art exists purely for its own beauty and value, without needing to serve moral, political, or social purposes.

Viewpoint:

- This idea was most famously promoted by 19th-century artists and writers like **Théophile Gautier**, **Oscar Wilde**, and **Walter Pater**.
- They rejected the idea that art should always teach a lesson or serve society.
- True art, they argued, was autonomous: its purpose was to create beauty, evoke emotion, and provide aesthetic experience — not to preach or persuade.

Example:

- **Oscar Wilde's** novel *The Picture of Dorian Gray* champions aestheticism but also plays with the irony that beautiful art can be morally ambiguous.
- **Gautier** insisted that art should be "useless" — that is, it should not be tied down by utility, politics, or morality.

Importance:

"Art for Art's Sake" freed artists from external demands and allowed a flowering of experimentation, modernism, and new, non-traditional forms of beauty.

Cultural Criticism

Meaning:

Cultural criticism is the practice of analyzing and evaluating culture (art, literature, media, and institutions) to uncover how it shapes society, reflects power structures, or perpetuates certain ideologies.

Viewpoint:

- Cultural critics examine how works of art influence and reflect social, political, and economic realities.
- Figures like **Matthew Arnold** (early cultural criticism) and later thinkers like **Theodor Adorno**, **Raymond Williams**, and **Edward Said** used cultural criticism to explore how art participates in broader cultural debates.
- Criticism involves questioning whose values are being promoted in art and whether art challenges or supports the status quo.

Example:

- **Arnold's***Culture and Anarchy* argued that culture (including art and literature) was a tool for human perfection and should stand against materialism and vulgarity.
- In the 20th century, **Marxist critics** analyzed how capitalist ideologies were hidden in seemingly neutral cultural products.

Importance:

Cultural criticism deepens our understanding of art's role in society, showing that even "pure" art is influenced by — and influences — political and social forces.

Main Contributions:

- **Matthew Arnold** (1822–1888)

  - In *The Study of Poetry*, Arnold elevated poetry as a superior form of moral and cultural education.
  - Proposed the concept of **"high seriousness"** — great literature should deal with profound moral issues.
  - Advocated that literature should replace religion as a guide to life.

- **John Ruskin** (1819–1900)

  - In works like *Modern Painters* and *The Stones of Venice*, Ruskin emphasized the connection between beauty, truth, and morality.
  - Argued that art must reflect moral truth and social concerns.

- **Walter Pater** (1839–1894)

  - In *The Renaissance*, Pater championed **"Art for Art's Sake"**, proposing that the aim of art is not to instruct but to provide aesthetic pleasure.
  - His aestheticism influenced writers like Oscar Wilde.

V

Chapter 5: Modern Literary Theories (20th Century Onward)

Section 5.1: Formalism

Overview:

Formalism focuses purely on the form and structure of literary works — analyzing *how* something is said rather than *what* is said.

Major Schools:

- **Russian Formalism** (1910s–1930s)
- **New Criticism** (1930s–1960s)

Key Concepts:

- **Defamiliarization** (making the familiar strange)
- **Close Reading**
- **Unity and Organic Form**

Defamiliarization (Making the Familiar Strange)

Defamiliarization is a concept that originates from Russian Formalist literary theory, particularly from the work of Viktor Shklovsky. It refers to the technique of presenting something in a way that makes it seem strange or unfamiliar, even though it is something we encounter regularly. The goal of defamiliarization is to encourage the reader or viewer to experience the world with fresh eyes, as if seeing something ordinary for the first time.This technique works by breaking the habitual patterns of perception, forcing the audience to reconsider their assumptions and view things in a more thoughtful or creative way. In literature, this can be achieved through unusual language, unusual perspectives, or by describing everyday objects or scenes in an unconventional manner.

For example:

- Instead of describing a common object like a cup simply as "a cup," a writer might describe its texture, weight, color, and shape in a way that makes us think about the cup's existence in a new way. This can force us to reconsider the purpose and meaning of everyday things that we might usually take for granted.

Close Reading

Close reading is a method of literary analysis that focuses on careful, detailed examination of a text, often with an emphasis on the nuances of language, structure, and meaning. The purpose of close reading is to extract deeper

understanding from the text itself, rather than relying on outside context or interpretation.
This method involves focusing on:

- **Language choices**: How does the author use particular words or phrases? Are there patterns in the diction? Is there symbolism or metaphor?
- **Structure**: How is the text organized? What is the effect of its structure on the meaning of the work?
- **Tone and style**: What is the author's attitude toward the subject or audience, and how is this conveyed through style?
- **Form**: How does the structure (e.g., verse, paragraph, sentence structure) influence the overall meaning?

- **Unity and Organic Form**

Unity and organic form are ideas often associated with the structure of a work of art or literature. These concepts are closely linked to the notion of how all parts of a work come together to create a cohesive and harmonious whole.

- **Unity** refers to the way in which all elements of a work (whether characters, themes, settings, etc.) work together to support the central idea or purpose. A unified work is one where all the parts feel interconnected and relevant to the overall theme or message. There should be no extraneous elements that seem out of place or disconnected from the rest of the piece.
- **Organic form** is a more specific idea that emphasizes that the structure of a work should grow naturally from its content, rather than being imposed externally. This means that the form of the work (its structure or organization) should feel like a natural extension of the material, rather than something artificially constructed. An organic work of art or literature "evolves" or "grows" from its elements and reflects the themes or subject matter it addresses.

For example:

- In literature, a novel with organic form would have a plot that evolves from the motivations and decisions of its characters. The structure wouldn't feel forced or artificially structured, but rather a natural progression of events.
- In visual arts, organic form might involve using shapes and lines that appear to grow or emerge naturally from the work itself, such as in certain naturalistic styles of painting.

Major Thinkers:

- **Viktor Shklovsky** (Russian Formalism)

  ○ Introduced **defamiliarization** — the artistic technique of presenting common things in unfamiliar ways to renew perception.

- **Cleanth Brooks** (New Criticism)

  ○ Advocated for **close reading** of texts without considering authorial intention or historical context.
  ○ Famous concepts: **The Heresy of Paraphrase** and **The Well-Wrought Urn**

- **I.A. Richards** (New Criticism)

○ In *Practical Criticism*, Richards emphasized reading poems without prior knowledge to focuspurely on the text.

Section 5.2: Structuralism
Overview:
Structuralism sees literature as a system of signs governed by underlying rules, much like language.
Major Thinkers:

- **Ferdinand de Saussure**
- **Claude Lévi-Strauss**
- **Roland Barthes**

Key Concepts:

- **Signifier and Signified** (Saussure)
- **Myth as a Language System** (Lévi-Strauss)
- **Writerly vs. Readerly Texts** (Barthes)

Signifier and Signified (Ferdinand de Saussure)

Swiss linguist Ferdinand de Saussure introduced the idea that a "sign" is made oftwo parts:

- **Signifier**: The physical form of a word, like its sound or written appearance (e.g., the word "tree").
- **Signified**: The mental concept or image linked to that word (e.g., the idea of a tree with leaves and branches).

The connection between the two is **arbitrary**—there's no natural reason why a word represents a concept. Instead, language gains meaning through the differences between signs.

Myth as a Language System (Claude Lévi-Strauss)

Claude Lévi-Strauss viewed myths as a system of signs, similar to language. He argued that myths create meaning through the relationships between elements like characters, themes, and symbols, not just through their stories. Myths are structured by binary oppositions—such as good/evil, life/death, and nature/culture—which reflect how language operates through differences.

Lévi-Strauss believed that myths across cultures share a universal "grammar," revealing deeper cultural and cognitive patterns. For example, the common hero-villain opposition symbolizes broader societal structures.

Ultimately, myths function as a language system, using symbolic structures to communicate ideas about human life, culture, and society, much like words and sentences convey meaning in language.

Writerly vs. Readerly Texts (Roland Barthes)

Roland Barthes, a French literary theorist, introduced the concepts of *writerly* and *readerly* texts in his essay "The Death of the Author" and other works. These concepts relate to how a text is created and how the reader interacts with it.

- **Readerly Texts**: These are texts that are more traditional in nature. They are closed and fixed, guiding the reader towards a single, clear interpretation. A reader of a readerly text simply receives the meaning that is given, passively interpreting the text according to the author's intentions or the established narrative structure.

  - Example: A conventional novel with a clear plot, defined characters, and a resolution is a readerly text. The reader consumes the text in a straightforward way, with little space for personal interpretation or interaction.

- **Writerly Texts**: In contrast, writerly texts are texts that are open, fragmented, and often non-linear. They require active participation from the reader, who must engage with the text in a more creative way, interpreting it, constructing meaning, and often filling in gaps. A writerly text doesn't offer a clear, predefined meaning but instead invites the reader to co-create meaning with the author.

- ◦ Example: Works like James Joyce's *Ulysses* or texts that are experimental in nature are often considered writerly. The reader must work harder to interpret the meaning, sometimes questioning the traditional boundaries of narrative and structure.

Main Contributions:

- **Saussure** (1857–1913)

  - ◦ Distinguished between **langue** (language system) and **parole** (individual utterance).
  - ◦ Language is a system of differences without positive terms.

- **Roland Barthes** (1915–1980)

  - ◦ In *Mythologies*, Barthes analyzed popular culture as systems of signs.
  - ◦ In *S/Z*, distinguished between **readerly** (passive) and **writerly** (active, interpretive) texts.

Section 5.3: Post-Structuralism / Deconstruction
Overview:
Post-structuralism challenges the idea of fixed meanings, suggesting that meanings are unstable and texts have endless interpretations.
Major Thinkers:

- **Jacques Derrida**
- **Michel Foucault**

Key Concepts:

- **Différance** (Derrida)
- **Death of the Author** (Barthes)
- **Power/Knowledge Relationship** (Foucault)

Différance (Jacques Derrida)

Derrida coined the term *différance* to explain a central aspect of his theory of deconstruction. *Différance* is a French term that Derrida created by blending the meanings of the verb "to differ" and "to defer." It refers to the way meaning is bothshaped by difference and postponed through time, creating an endless chain of interpretations.

Here's a more detailed explanation:

- **Difference**: In any linguistic system, words or signs acquire their meaning not because of a direct, inherent link to the world or reality, but because they differ from other words or signs. For example, the word "dog" means what it does because it is not "cat," "bird," or any other word. This system of differences is what constructs meaning.
- **Deferral**: Meaning is also always *deferred*, meaning that it is never fully present or fixed. Whenever we try to define something, we always have to refer to other signs or words to clarify its meaning, and those other signs lead to further references, creating an infinite chain. Therefore, meaning is always in a state of becoming—it is never fully stabilized.

Derrida used *différance* to challenge the traditional understanding of meaning, suggesting that it is always unstable and in flux. In his deconstructionist approach, Derrida argued that texts are always open to multiple interpretations, and this endless play of meanings prevents any final, determinate interpretation from being established.

In essence, *différance* reveals that meaning is not something fixed or intrinsic but is always dependent on context, relationships, and temporal shifts.

Death of the Author (Roland Barthes)

In his essay *The Death of the Author* (1967), Roland Barthes argues that the identity and intentions of the author should not influence or limit the interpretation of a text. According to Barthes, the author's personal biography, intentions, or presumed messages should not be the primary way we read and interpret a text. Instead, meaning should be derived from the text itself and the interaction between the reader and the text.

Here's a detailed look at Barthes' argument:

- **Traditional View of Authorship**: In traditional literary theory, the author's intentions and background were considered central to understanding a text. Readers were encouraged to look for clues within the text that reflected the author's personal experiences, thoughts, and beliefs.

- **The Death of the Author**: Barthes challenges this view by asserting that the moment a text is created and shared with the public, the author's control over its meaning ends. The text exists independently of the author's identity or intentions. In this sense, Barthes metaphorically declares the "death" of the author: the reader is no longer bound by the author's personal context but is free to interpret the text on their own terms.

- **The Role of the Reader**: Barthes places emphasis on the role of the reader, arguing that the act of reading and interpreting is an active process. The reader creates meaning by interacting with the text, and different readers may interpret the same text in multiple ways. Barthes' view allows for a more democratic and fluid relationship between the reader and the text, where meaning is not dictated by the author but emerges from the reader's engagement with the work.

In short, the "Death of the Author" calls for a shift in how we understand texts. It undermines the authority of the author, suggesting that meaning is not fixed by the author's intentions but is created in the space between the text and the reader.

Power/Knowledge Relationship (Michel Foucault)

Michel Foucault explored the interconnection between power and knowledge in his work. He argued that power and knowledge are deeply intertwined, and that knowledge is not something neutral but is shaped by power relations within society. The concept of "Power/Knowledge" suggests that power is not just exercised through political institutions or force, but also through the production and control of knowledge.

Here's a more detailed explanation:

- **Knowledge is Power**: Foucault argued that knowledge is never purely objective or impartial. Instead, the production of knowledge is influenced by power structures. Institutions (such as schools, hospitals, prisons, or governments) determine what counts as legitimate knowledge and what does not, and in doing so, they shape social norms, behaviors, and beliefs.

- **Power is Embedded in Knowledge**: Power is not just something that is exerted from the top down by authority figures; rather, it is diffused throughout society and is embedded in the production and dissemination of knowledge. For instance, the medical field has the power to define what constitutes normal or abnormal health, and this knowledge is used to regulate behaviors and attitudes about health and illness.

- **Disciplinary Power**: Foucault is particularly interested in how power operates through institutions that manage and regulate individuals' bodies and behaviors. In his works like *Discipline and Punish*, he explores how disciplinary institutions like prisons and schools exert control by shaping knowledge about individuals, categorizing them, and making them conform to societal norms.

- **The Relationship between Power and Knowledge**: Foucault argues that power and knowledge are inextricably linked. Knowledge is not something that exists outside of power, nor is power something that operates without knowledge. Instead, they produce and sustain each other. For example, the medical profession produces knowledge about the human body, and in turn, this knowledge allows medical professionals to exercise power over individuals by diagnosing, categorizing, and prescribing treatments.

- **Knowledge as a Tool of Control**: In Foucault's view, knowledge serves as a tool for social control. The way knowledge is constructed influences who has power and how that power is exercised. Institutions use knowledge to categorize, normalize, and control individuals. This can be seen in various practices, such as the way the legal system uses legal knowledge to structure justice or how educational institutions use knowledge to dictate what students learn.

Bottom of Form**Main Contributions:**

- **Jacques Derrida** (1930–2004)

  - In *Of Grammatology*, Derrida introduced **deconstruction** — a method of exposing internal contradictions in a text.
  - Language always defers meaning; there is no final, fixed interpretation.

- **Michel Foucault** (1926–1984)

  - Explored the relationship between **power** and **knowledge** in shaping discourse.
  - In works like *Discipline and Punish*, showed how systems of power control society through language and practices.

Section 5.4: Psychoanalytic Criticism
Overview:
Psychoanalytic criticism applies theories of psychology to literature, focusing on unconscious desires, anxieties, and conflicts.
Major Thinkers:Sigmund Freud, Jacques Lacan
Key Concepts:

- **Oedipus Complex**
- **Unconscious Desire**
- **Mirror Stage** (Lacan)

Oedipus complex (Sigmund Freud)

The **Oedipus complex** is a concept by Sigmund Freud describing a child's unconscious desire for the opposite-sex parent and rivalry with the same-sex parent. It appears during the **phallic stage** of development (ages 3–6). Boys develop affection for their mother and jealousy toward their father, along with **castration anxiety** (fear of punishment). Girls experience a similar process, called the **Electra complex**, involving desire for their father and **penis envy**, though Freud's explanation for girls was less clear.

Resolution happens when the child identifies with the same-sex parent and adopts societal roles and norms. Freud believed unresolved oedipal feelings could cause adult problems like guilt, relationship issues, and authority conflicts. Although the theory is now debated and criticized for

its gender bias and limited scope, the Oedipus Complex remains one of Freud's most famous and influential ideas.

Unconscious Desire (Sigmund Freud)

Unconscious desire is a key idea in Freud's psychoanalysis. Freud believed much of our behavior, thoughts, and emotions are driven by hidden desires rooted in early childhood.

The **unconscious mind** holds repressed memories and feelings that are too disturbing or unacceptable to be conscious. These hidden desires appear in **dreams, Freudian slips**, and **neurotic symptoms.**

Repression keeps socially or morally unacceptable desires out of awareness, but they still influence behavior. Freud emphasized that **sexual (libido)** and **aggressive (Thanatos)** drives mainly fuel these unconscious forces.

In therapy, **free association** helps uncover repressed desires, leading to greater insight and healing. Freud's idea of unconscious desire also influenced fields like **literature, art, and cultural studies**, highlighting its broad impact on understanding human behavior.

Mirror Stage (Jacques Lacan)

The **Mirror Stage**, introduced by Jacques Lacan, describes a key moment in early childhood (around 6–18 months) when a child first recognizes themselves in a mirror. This recognition creates the sense of an **"I"** or ego, but it is also a **misrecognition**—the child sees a unified image that doesn't match their still-fragmented bodily experience.

The **mirror image** becomes the basis for the ego's lifelong desire for unity and coherence, even though true unity is unattainable. The Mirror Stage also marks the start of the child's awareness of the **Other** (external world) and their entry into the **Symbolic Order**—the world of language and social structures.

For Lacan, this early misrecognition shapes the human experience of identity, desire, and anxiety throughout life.

Main Contributions:

- **Sigmund Freud** (1856–1939)

  - Literature expresses unconscious drives.
  - Analysis of dreams and symbolism crucial in interpreting texts.

- **Jacques Lacan** (1901–1981)

  - Proposed that identity is formed through the **Mirror Stage** — recognition of self as an "other."
  - Emphasized the importance of language (the Symbolic Order) in shaping the unconscious.

Section 5.5: Marxist Criticism

Overview:

Marxist criticism sees literature as a reflection or critique of the material, economic realities of its time.

Major Thinkers:

- **Karl Marx**
- **Raymond Williams**
- **Terry Eagleton**

Key Concepts:

- **Base and Superstructure Ideology**
- **Cultural Materialism**

Base and Superstructure (Karl Marx)

The **Base and Superstructure** model is a foundational concept in Marxist theory. Marx used it to describe the relationship between a society's economic system (*the base*) and its cultural, legal, political, and ideological life (*the superstructure*).

Detailed explanation:

- **Base**:
The base refers to the economic foundation of society. It includes:

  - The **forces of production** (technology, labor, natural resources).
  - The **relations of production** (class relationships, such as between workers and owners, or serfs and lords).

The base determines how goods are produced and how society organizes labor and resources. It is the material reality of life.

- **Superstructure**:
The superstructure arises from and is shaped by the base. It includes:

  - **Politics** (government, laws, political institutions).
  - **Culture** (art, religion, philosophy, education, media, etc.).
  - **Ideology** (ideas and beliefs about society, morality, justice, etc.).

The superstructure serves to justify, maintain, and sometimes mask the realities of the base. For example, religious or political ideas might legitimize the economic dominance of one class over another.

- **Relationship Between Base and Superstructure**:

  - The base **shapes** the superstructure. That means economic conditions deeply influence a society's ideas, culture, and institutions.
  - In turn, the superstructure can **reinforce** and **stabilize** the base, maintaining the status quo and discouraging revolution.

Example: In a capitalist society, the economy (base) emphasizes private ownership and profit. This economic reality influences political systems (democracy structured to protect property) and cultural beliefs (ideas about individualism and competition).

Ideology

Ideology refers to systems of beliefs that shape how people see the world, often benefiting dominant groups without their awareness. **Marx** viewed ideology as a distortion that masks exploitation, creating **false consciousness** among workers who misinterpret their real conditions. **Althusser** expanded this idea, arguing that ideology is a **material force** spread through **Ideological State Apparatuses** (schools, media, family) that shape individuals' views and behaviors unconsciously.

Key features:

- Ideology feels natural but is historically constructed.
- It maintains social hierarchies and resists change.

Example: The belief that "hard work guarantees success" supports capitalism by blaming poverty on individuals rather than systemic inequality.

Cultural Materialism (Raymond Williams and Others)

Cultural Materialism is an approach developed in Britain in the 1970s and 1980s by critics like **Raymond Williams**, **Jonathan Dollimore**, and **Alan Sinfield**. It blends Marxist theory with literary and cultural criticism, focusing on how culture is materially embedded in everyday life and power structures.

Detailed explanation:

- **Key Principles**:

  - Culture is not just a reflection of society (*superstructure*)—it is an active part of material life, intertwined with economic and political realities.
  - Literary and cultural works are **sites of struggle** where dominant (hegemonic) and resistant (counter-hegemonic) ideas clash.
  - Critics should study both **"high" culture** (like Shakespeare) and **"popular" culture** (like soap operas, music, etc.) to understand power relations.

- **Four Focus Areas (Graham Holderness summarized Cultural Materialism this way)**:

  - **Historical Context**: Understand texts in their original historical and political settings.
  - **Political Commitment**: Criticism should be politically engaged and aware of present-day struggles.
  - **Theoretical Method**: Use theory (especially Marxism, feminism, post colonialism) to analyze culture.
  - **Textual Analysis**: Close reading of cultural texts, seeing them as part of material social practices.
  - **Raymond Williams' Contribution**:
    Williams rejected the strict Base/Superstructure model that placed culture entirely as a "reflection" of economics. Instead, he argued that culture is **material** and **active**, part of shaping social reality, not just passively shaped by it.
  - **Example**:
    Studying *Shakespeare's plays* through Cultural Materialism would involve:

  - Asking how the plays reflect and reinforce Elizabethan political power.
  - Asking how modern performances reinterpret Shakespeare for new political purposes (e.g., feminist or anti-colonial readings).

  Main Contributions:

- **Karl Marx** (1818–1883)

  - Society's economic base influences its cultural superstructure.
  - Art is both a product and a critique of historical forces.

- **Raymond Williams** (1921–1988)

  - Focused on the relationship between culture and society.
  - Emphasized "structures of feeling" — lived experience shaping culture.

- **Terry Eagleton** (b. 1943)

  - In *Literary Theory: An Introduction*, Eagleton critiques traditional literary studies from a Marxist standpoint.

  Section 5.6: Feminist Criticism
  Overview:
Feminist criticism examines literature through the lens of gender, questioning traditional patriarchal assumptions.
  Major Thinkers:

- **Simone de Beauvoir**
- **Elaine Showalter**

- **Judith Butler**

Key Concepts:

○ **Gynocriticism** (study of women writers)
○ **Gender Performativity** (Butler)

Gynocriticism (Study of Women Writers)
Originator:

- Coined by **Elaine Showalter** in her essay *"Towards a Feminist Poetics"* (1979).

Definition:
Gynocriticism is the critical practice focused on **studying women's writing**—not as an offshoot or response to male literary traditions, but as a distinct literary tradition of its own. It aims to **create a female framework** for the analysis of women's literature, exploring the experiences, themes, and language unique to women authors.
Purpose:

- Move away from male-centered literary criticism (which often treated women's writing as derivative or secondary).
- Understand the **"woman as producer of textual meaning"**, not just as a character or subject.
- Build a **female literary history**, looking at how women's experiences shape their writing.

Key Focus Areas in Gynocriticism:

- **Themes** common in women's literature (e.g., identity, confinement, sexuality, domestic life).
- **Forms and genres** favored by women writers (diaries, letters, novels, etc.).
- **Language and style**: Does women's writing have a unique linguistic style?
- **Psychological and cultural conditions** affecting women's creativity (e.g., repression, education, societal expectations).

Three Stages of Women's Literary Development (Showalter's Model):

1. **Feminine Phase (1840–1880):** Women writers imitate male norms and styles.
2. **Feminist Phase (1880–1920):** Women protest against male literary standards and advocate for rights.
3. **Female Phase (1920–present):** Women explore female experience authentically without reference to male norms.

Impact:
Gynocriticism helped to **recover forgotten women writers**, challenged patriarchal literary history, and paved the way for more nuanced feminist literary theories.
Gender Performativity (Judith Butler)
Originator:

- Introduced by **Judith Butler** in her book *"Gender Trouble"* (1990).

Definition:
Gender performativity is the idea that **gender is not something one is**, but **something one does**—a **series of acts, gestures, and behaviors** repeated over time. It's not an inner truth or essence but rather **an effect produced by**

performance.
Main Ideas:

- **Gender is constructed**: It's not biologically innate; society teaches individuals how to act "male" or "female."
- **Performance is compulsory**: People are compelled by cultural norms to act according to gender roles, often unconsciously.
- **No original gender identity exists**: Gender is always an imitation of societal norms; there is no "true" gender to imitate.
- **Subversion is possible**: Since gender is performative, individuals can disrupt gender norms through alternative performances (e.g., drag shows, gender non-conforming behaviors).

Key Quotes from Butler:

- *"There is no gender identity behind the expressions of gender; that identity is performatively constituted by the very 'expressions' that are said to be its results."*
- *"Gender is a kind of imitation for which there is no original."*

Example:

When a person dresses, speaks, and behaves in ways associated with "femininity" or "masculinity," they are performing gender. These performances create the **illusion** of a stable gender identity, but they are **cultural constructs**.
Implications:

- Challenges binary understandings of male/female, masculine/feminine.
- Influences queer theory, transgender studies, and contemporary feminist thought.
- Suggests that changing performances can lead to broader social change in understanding gender.

Main Contributions:

- **Simone de Beauvoir** (1908–1986)

  - In *The Second Sex*, argues that "One is not born, but rather becomes, a woman," highlighting societal construction of gender roles.

- **Elaine Showalter** (b. 1941)

  - Advocated **Gynocriticism**: studying women's writing as its own tradition rather than through male-centered theories.

- **Judith Butler** (b. 1956)

  - In *Gender Trouble*, introduced the idea that gender is not innate but performed through repeated actions.

Section 5.7: Postcolonial Criticism
Overview:

Postcolonial criticism analyzes the impact of colonialism on cultures and literatures, questioning Eurocentric perspectives.
Major Thinkers:

- **Edward Said**
- **Homi Bhabha**
- **Gayatri Chakravorty Spivak**

Key Concepts:

- **Orientalism** (Said)
- **Hybridity** (Bhabha)
- **Subaltern Studies** (Spivak)

Orientalism — *Edward Said*
Source:

- Book: *Orientalism* (1978)

Definition:
Orientalism refers to the **Western style of dominating, restructuring, and having authority over the East** (Asia, the Middle East, etc.). According to Said, the "Orient" is **a constructed image**—a set of stereotypes invented by the West to justify colonial domination.
Key Ideas:

- **Representation as Power:** Western scholars, writers, and artists have historically portrayed the East as exotic, backward, irrational, sensual, and dangerous, thus **justifying imperialism.**
- **The Orient as 'Other':** The West (Occident) defines itself as **rational, moral, and superior** by contrasting itself with the "inferior" East.
- **Knowledge = Power:** Academic and literary knowledge about the East wasn't innocent; it was part of the political project of control. **"Knowledge about the Orient is never separate from power over it."**

- **Cultural Imperialism:** Even without direct political control, the West exercises **cultural dominance** through representation, media, literature, and scholarship.

Important Quote:
"Orientalism can be discussed and analyzed as the corporate institution for dealing with the Orient — dealing with it by making statements about it, authorizing views of it, describing it, by teaching it, settling it, ruling over it."
Impact:

- Revolutionized postcolonial studies.
- Challenged Eurocentric views in academia.
- Inspired critical re-readings of Western representations of non-Western societies.

Hybridity — *Homi K. Bhabha*

Source:

- Book: *The Location of Culture* (1994)

Definition:
Hybridity refers to the **mixing of cultures, identities, and languages** that happens when colonial and colonized cultures meet. It creates **new, "in-between" identities** that are **neither purely colonial nor purely native.**

Key Ideas:

- **Cultural Mixing:** Colonialism was not a one-way imposition. Colonized subjects absorbed, altered, and transformed colonial culture, creating **hybrid identities.**
- **Third Space:** The hybrid identity exists in what Bhabha calls the **Third Space** — a space of negotiation where new cultural meanings are formed.
- **Subversion of Authority:** Hybridity can **undermine colonial authority**, because colonized people mimic colonial culture but with difference, exposing its instability.
- **Mimicry:** A related concept where colonized subjects imitate colonial behaviors, but never perfectly, producing **"almost the same, but not quite"** versions that destabilize colonial dominance.

Important Quote:
"It is in the emergence of the interstices—the overlap and displacement of domains of difference—that the intersubjective and collective experiences of nationness, community interest, or cultural value are negotiated."
Impact:

- Changed the way postcolonial identity is understood.
- Emphasized fluidity and negotiation rather than rigid binaries (colonizer/colonized).

Subaltern Studies — *Gayatri Chakravorty Spivak*
Source:

- Influenced by the *Subaltern Studies Group* (Ranajit Guha and others).
- Key essay: *"Can the Subaltern Speak?"* (1988)

Definition:
The **subaltern** refers to **marginalized groups** outside the power structures of colonial and postcolonial society — those who are so oppressed that they cannot **speak** or be **heard** in dominant discourse.
Key Ideas:

- **Silenced Voices:** Subalterns (especially poor, rural, female populations) have no voice in the dominant historical narrative.
- **Representation Problems:** Even when intellectuals (Western or elite local) try to "speak for" the subaltern, they risk **reproducing the same structures of domination.**
- **Critique of Western Intellectuals:** Spivak critiques thinkers like Foucault and Deleuze, arguing that their theories often ignore the **real, lived conditions of the subaltern.**
- **"Can the Subaltern Speak?":** Spivak's answer is largely **no** — because the structures of power silence them.

Important Quote:
"The subaltern cannot speak. There is no virtue in global laundry lists with 'woman' as a pious item."
Impact:

- Transformed postcolonial theory by focusing on **those most invisible.**
- Critiqued both Western and Indian elite approaches to history and identity.
- Brought attention to intersections of **gender, class, and colonialism.**

Main Contributions:

- **Edward Said** (1935–2003)

In *Orientalism*, Said argued that the West constructed the East as an exotic, inferior "Other" to justify colonial domination.

- **Homi K. Bhabha** (b. 1949)

  ○ Emphasized concepts of **hybridity** and **mimicry**, showing how colonial subjects resist colonial authority.

- **Gayatri Chakravorty Spivak** (b. 1942)

  ○ In "Can the Subaltern Speak?", questioned whether marginalized people can truly have a voice under oppressive systems.

Section 5.8: Ecocriticism
Overview:
Ecocriticism examines the relationship between literature and the environment, considering how texts represent nature and ecological concerns.
Key Concepts:

- **Anthropocentrism** (human-centered thinking)
- **Deep Ecology**
- **Environmental Justice**

Anthropocentrism (Human-Centered Thinking)
Anthropocentrism is the belief that humans are the most important beings in the universe. It sees nature mainly as something useful for human needs.
Key points:

- Nature is valued for what it gives humans (like food, materials, and fun).
- Humans are seen as superior to animals, plants, and ecosystems.
- Nature is often treated as something to control and use.
- This mindset has led to problems like climate change, deforestation, and species extinction.

Criticism:
Many environmental thinkers say anthropocentrism causes ecological damage. They suggest we should value all life, not just human life.
Example:
Clearing forests for farming without caring about wildlife or the environment.
Deep Ecology
Deep Ecology is an idea from Arne Næss (1973) that says all living things are important, not just humans. It teaches us to respect nature and live in a simpler, less harmful way.
Main ideas:

- Every living thing deserves to live.
- Humans are just a small part of nature.

- We should have fewer people, use fewer resources, and change how we live.

- Real happiness comes from feeling connected to the Earth.

Deep Ecology beliefs:

- Life is valuable by itself.
- A variety of life makes the world better.
- We should only harm nature if it's truly needed.
- Big changes in how we live and run society are needed.
- People who believe this should help make changes.

Criticism:
Some say Deep Ecology is too extreme and ignores human problems like poverty.
Example:
Fighting against building a dam because it hurts animals and nature, not just people.

Environmental Justice

Environmental Justice is the idea that everyone—no matter their race, income, or background—deserves a safe and healthy environment.
Key ideas:

- Environmental problems like pollution often harm poor and minority communities more.
- Environmental issues are also human rights issues.
- Everyone should be included in making environmental decisions.
- Focus areas: pollution, clean water, safe housing, climate justice, indigenous rights.

History:
The movement grew in the 1980s in the U.S., starting with protests against toxic waste dumps in African American neighborhoods (like Warren County, NC).
Important beliefs:

- Protecting the Earth is a basic human right.
- Opposing harmful corporate actions.
- Making policies based on respect for all people.

Example:
Fighting against hazardous landfills near Native American or African American communities.

CONCLUSION

Literary theory offers not only a set of tools for interpreting texts but also a rich intellectual history of how humans have understood language, culture, and meaning across centuries. From the earliest speculations of Plato and Aristotle about the nature and purpose of art, through the ordered rationalism of the Neoclassical age, the passionate rebellion of the Romantics, and the socially concerned critiques of the Victorians, to the dizzying array of modern and postmodern theories, literature has remained a site of endless exploration, debate, and innovation.

Each theoretical movement we have explored — from Formalism's close reading of the text itself to Structuralism's search for underlying systems, from Marxism's analysis of socio-economic structures to Feminism's critique of patriarchal norms, from Postcolonialism's study of empire to Ecocriticism's urgent engagement with the environment — demonstrates that literature is not an isolated aesthetic object but a living, dynamic part of the human experience. Theory has taught us that texts do not have a single, fixed meaning, but instead participate in networks of meaning that shift depending on readers, contexts, and histories.

In todays globalized, digitized, and ecologically challenged world, literary theory remains more vital than ever. It helps readers cultivate critical thinking, question dominant narratives, and empathize with diverse perspectives. It invites us to interrogate how identities are constructed, how power operates in subtle ways, and how language shapes our reality. Understanding literary theory equips students, scholars, and general readers alike with the means to not merely consume culture, but to engage with it critically and creatively.

Moreover, literary theory bridges disciplines — philosophy, sociology, psychology, political science, environmental studies — reflecting the inherently interdisciplinary nature of human knowledge. It reminds us that literature cannot be fully understood without considering the worlds — historical, political, social, and psychological — that both produce and are produced by it.

This book aimed to offer an accessible yet comprehensive overview of the major literary theories relevant to students preparing for competitive examinations and aspiring scholars. By mastering these theories, readers will not only perform better academically but will also develop richer, more nuanced ways of reading and thinking about the world.

As you continue your journey through the study of literature, remember that theory is not meant to limit your interpretations but to expand them. It provides the vocabulary and frameworks necessary for deeper exploration, allowing you to ask new questions and discover new meanings.

The greatest reward of studying literary theory is the realization that meaning is not static but endlessly generative — and that every act of reading is an act of creation.

Happy Reading and Critical Thinking!

Glossary Of Literary Terms

A

Anthropocentrism — The belief that human beings are the central or most significant entities, often critiqued by ecocriticism for marginalizing nature.

B

Base and Superstructure — In Marxist theory, the "base" refers to the economic foundation of society, while the "superstructure" comprises its culture, ideology, and institutions, which are shaped by the base.

C

Catharsis — In Aristotle's *Poetics*, the emotional purification or cleansing experienced by the audience of a tragedy through feelings of pity and fear.

Close Reading — Careful, detailed analysis of the text itself, focusing on structure, language, and meaning without external context.

Cultural Materialism — A Marxist approach focusing on the material conditions that shape culture, highlighting power relations in society.

D

Decorum — The classical principle that literary style should be appropriate to the subject matter and character, emphasized by Horace.

Defamiliarization — The technique of making familiar objects or ideas seem strange to refresh perception, introduced by Viktor Shklovsky.

Différance — Derrida's concept indicating that meaning is always deferred in language, making fixed interpretation impossible.

E

Environmental Justice — A concept in ecocriticism promoting fair treatment and involvement of all people in environmental policies.

G

Gender Performativity — Judith Butler's idea that gender is not innate but performed through repeated behaviors and actions.

Gynocriticism — A feminist critical practice that studies the writing of women as a distinct literary tradition, advanced by Elaine Showalter.

H

High Seriousness — Matthew Arnold's idea that great literature should address profound moral and intellectual concerns.

Hybridity — Homi Bhabha's concept in postcolonial theory describing the blending of colonial and native cultures, creating new, resistant identities.

I

Imitation of Nature — A neoclassical principle that art should mirror the natural world, but with order and refinement.

L

Langue and Parole — Saussure's terms: *langue* refers to the overall structure of language, while *parole* refers to individual speech acts.

M

Mirror Stage — Jacques Lacan's theory that identity formation begins when a child recognizes its image in a mirror, forming the basis of the ego.

Mimesis — The representation or imitation of life and reality in art and literature, central to the theories of Plato and Aristotle.

Moral Function of Art — The belief, prominent in Victorian theory, that literature should promote ethical and cultural values.

Myth as a Language System — Claude Lévi-Strauss's idea that myths are structured like language, following deep, universal patterns.

O

Oedipus Complex — Freud's psychoanalytic concept where a child feels unconscious desire for the opposite-sex parent and rivalry with the same-sex parent.

Order and Balance — A neoclassical ideal emphasizing proportion, harmony, and restraint in literature.

Orientalism — Edward Said's term for the depiction of Eastern societies as exotic, backward, and inferior, used to justify Western imperialism.

P

Power/Knowledge Relationship — Foucault's idea that power and knowledge are intertwined, and control over knowledge systems shapes societal structures.

Primary Imagination — In Coleridge's *Biographia Literaria*, the spontaneous and unconscious creative power of the human mind.

Postcolonial Criticism — A critical approach that examines literature produced in the context of colonialism and its aftermath.

Post-Structuralism — A movement that challenges the idea of stable meanings and promotes the endless play of signification in texts.

Preface to Lyrical Ballads — William Wordsworth's foundational text for Romantic literary theory, emphasizing emotion and common language in poetry.

Psychoanalytic Criticism — An approach that applies theories of the unconscious mind to the interpretation of literature.

R

Readerly vs. Writerly Texts — Roland Barthes's distinction where *readerly* texts present fixed meanings, while *writerly* texts invite active interpretation.

S

Secondary Imagination — In Coleridge's theory, the conscious, artistic shaping of experience and perception.

Signifier and Signified — Saussure's terms in linguistics: the *signifier* is the form of a word or symbol; the *signified* is the concept it represents.

Sublimity — A quality of greatness or grandeur in literature that transcends ordinary experience, discussed by Longinus.

Subaltern — A term used by Gayatri Spivak to refer to marginalized populations excluded from dominant power structures.

Structuralism — A critical approach that views literature as part of a larger system governed by underlying rules and structures.

Structures of Feeling — Raymond Williams's concept of the lived experience of a particular time, shaping and shaped by culture.

T

The Death of the Author — Roland Barthes's idea that the author's intentions are irrelevant to the interpretation of a text.

Tragedy (Aristotelian) — A dramatic form characterized by serious action and the evocation of pity and fear leading to catharsis.

U

Unity and Organic Form — New Critical principles that a literary work should be seen as an organic whole, where every element contributes to the overall meaning.

Practice MCQs for Competitive Examinations

1. **Who is known for the concept of "mimesis" in classical literary theory?**

   - ◦ a) Aristotle
   - ◦ b) Plato
   - ◦ c) Horace
   - ◦ d) Samuel Taylor Coleridge
     Answer: b) Plato

2. **What does the concept of "catharsis" primarily refer to in Aristotle's theory?**

   - ◦ a) Emotional purification
   - ◦ b) Aesthetic enjoyment
   - ◦ c) Moral righteousness
   - ◦ d) Rational logic
     Answer: a) Emotional purification

3. **Which of the following is NOT one of the "unities" in Aristotle's poetics?**

   - ◦ a) Unity of place
   - ◦ b) Unity of time
   - ◦ c) Unity of action
   - ◦ d) Unity of character
     Answer: d) Unity of character

4. **According to Plato, what is the primary role of art in society?**

   - ◦ a) To reflect the ideals of truth and beauty
   - ◦ b) To imitate reality and promote virtue
   - ◦ c) To engage the emotions of the audience
   - ◦ d) To entertain and provide pleasure
     Answer: b) To imitate reality and promote virtue

5. **Which philosopher emphasized the importance of "tragedy" as a vehicle for catharsis?**

   - ◦ a) Horace
   - ◦ b) Aristotle
   - ◦ c) Plato
   - ◦ d) John Dryden
     Answer: b) Aristotle

6. **Which thinker is known for defining the principle of "decorum" in literary works?**

   - ◦ a) Horace

- ◦ b) Longinus
- ◦ c) Aristotle
- ◦ d) William Wordsworth
  Answer: a) Horace

7. **The concept of "the sublime" was central to which Neoclassical thinker?**

   - ◦ a) John Dryden
   - ◦ b) Longinus
   - ◦ c) Samuel Taylor Coleridge
   - ◦ d) Walter Pater
     Answer: b) Longinus

8. **Which of the following is NOT a characteristic of Neoclassical literature?**

   - ◦ a) Emphasis on order and harmony

   - ◦ b) Inspiration from ancient Greek and Roman texts
   - ◦ c) Focus on emotion and individual expression
   - ◦ d) Strict literary rules and norms
     Answer: c) Focus on emotion and individual expression

2. **Who is the author of "An Essay on Criticism," which outlines Neoclassical literary standards?**

   - ◦ a) Samuel Johnson
   - ◦ b) John Dryden
   - ◦ c) Alexander Pope
   - ◦ d) William Wordsworth
     Answer: c) Alexander Pope

3. **Which of the following did Neoclassical critics value most in literature?**

   - ◦ a) Reason and propriety
   - ◦ b) Imagination and fantasy
   - ◦ c) Spontaneity and freedom
   - ◦ d) Individualism and emotion
     Answer: a) Reason and propriety

4. **Which of the following Romantic poets focused on the concept of "poetic imagination"?**

   - ◦ a) John Keats
   - ◦ b) Samuel Taylor Coleridge
   - ◦ c) William Wordsworth
   - ◦ d) Percy Bysshe Shelley
     Answer: c) William Wordsworth

5. **Which Romantic poet believed that the poet is a "spiritual guide" for society?**

- ◦ a) Percy Bysshe Shelley
- ◦ b) Samuel Taylor Coleridge
- ◦ c) William Wordsworth
- ◦ d) Lord Byron
  Answer: a) Percy Bysshe Shelley

6. **Which concept is central to Romantic literary theory?**

   - ◦ a) The sublime
   - ◦ b) Rationality
   - ◦ c) Decorum
   - ◦ d) High seriousness
     Answer: a) The sublime

7. **Which of the following is a key theme in Romanticism?**

   - ◦ a) Emphasis on individualism and emotion
   - ◦ b) The importance of social order and propriety
   - ◦ c) Adherence to strict rules and norms
   - ◦ d) The rejection of nature as a source of inspiration
     Answer: a) Emphasis on individualism and emotion

8. **What is the focus of Romantic literary theory?**

   - ◦ a) Structure and form
   - ◦ b) Nature and the individual's emotional connection to it
   - ◦ c) Morality and social duty
   - ◦ d) Philosophical reasoning
     Answer: b) Nature and the individual's emotional connection to it

16. **Which Victorian critic focused on the role of literature in moral and cultural criticism?**

    - ◦ a) Walter Pater
    - ◦ b) John Ruskin
    - ◦ c) Matthew Arnold
    - ◦ d) T.S. Eliot
      Answer: c) Matthew Arnold

17. **What concept is central to John Ruskin's approach to art criticism?**

    - ◦ a) High seriousness
    - ◦ b) Art for art's sake
    - ◦ c) Cultural criticism
    - ◦ d) Aestheticism
      Answer: b) Art for art's sake

18. **Who argued that literature should be concerned with both beauty and moral instruction?**

- ◦ a) T.S. Eliot
- ◦ b) Matthew Arnold
- ◦ c) Walter Pater
- ◦ d) Samuel Taylor Coleridge
  Answer: b) Matthew Arnold

19. **Which of the following was a major concern of Victorian literary critics?**

- ◦ a) The role of art in shaping social and moral values
- ◦ b) The focus on the unconscious mind
- ◦ c) The rejection of social responsibility
- ◦ d) The pursuit of beauty above all else
  Answer: a) The role of art in shaping social and moral values

20. **What did Victorian critics like Walter Pater promote?**

- ◦ a) Art should serve as a moral guide
- ◦ b) Art is separate from morality and should be appreciated for its own sake
- ◦ c) Art should reflect the social norms of the time
- ◦ d) Art is irrelevant to human experience
  Answer: b) Art is separate from morality and should be appreciated for its own sake

21. **Which literary theory emphasizes the form and structure of literature?**

- ◦ a) Structuralism
- ◦ b) Formalism
- ◦ c) Post-Structuralism
- ◦ d) Marxism
  Answer: b) Formalism

22. **Who is a major proponent of Russian Formalism?**

- ◦ a) Viktor Shklovsky
- ◦ b) Jacques Derrida
- ◦ c) Ferdinand de Saussure
- ◦ d) Terry Eagleton
  Answer: a) Viktor Shklovsky

23. **What is a key focus of Formalist criticism?**

- ◦ a) The author's intention
- ◦ b) Historical context

- ◦ c) The language and technique of the text
- ◦ d) The moral message of the text
  Answer: c) The language and technique of the text

24. **Which of the following is NOT associated with Formalist criticism?**

- ◦ a) The importance of narrative structure
- ◦ b) Focus on the psychological depth of characters
- ◦ c) Analysis of imagery and symbols
- ◦ d) Close reading of the text's form
  Answer: b) Focus on the psychological depth of characters

25. **Cleanth Brooks is most closely associated with which literary theory?**

- ◦ a) Structuralism
- ◦ b) Formalism
- ◦ c) Psychoanalytic Criticism
- ◦ d) Marxist Criticism
  Answer: b) Formalism

26. **Which theorist is considered the father of Structuralism?**

- ◦ a) Roland Barthes
- ◦ b) Ferdinand de Saussure
- ◦ c) Michel Foucault
- ◦ d) Jacques Derrida
  Answer: b) Ferdinand de Saussure

27. **In Structuralism, what is a key concept regarding language?**

- ◦ a) The instability of meaning
- ◦ b) The importance of binary oppositions
- ◦ c) The role of the individual in interpreting texts
- ◦ d) The fixed relationship between words and meaning
  Answer: b) The importance of binary oppositions

28. **Which of the following is a characteristic of Structuralist criticism?**

- ◦ a) Focus on individual author intention
- ◦ b) Examination of how texts are part of larger cultural systems
- ◦ c) Study of the emotional impact of literature
- ◦ d) Rejection of formal elements of a text
  Answer: b) Examination of how texts are part of larger cultural systems

29. **What term did Roland Barthes introduce to describe the process of creating meaning in a text?**

- ◦ a) The death of the author
- ◦ b) The signifier-signified relationship
- ◦ c) Structural analysis
- ◦ d) The mirror stage
  Answer: a) The death of the author

30. **Which structuralist concept refers to the relationship between the signifier and the signified?**

- ◦ a) Binary oppositions
- ◦ b) Signification
- ◦ c) Intertextuality
- ◦ d) Semiology
  Answer: b) Signification

31. **Who is the primary figure associated with Deconstruction?**

    - ◦ a) Jacques Derrida
    - ◦ b) Michel Foucault
    - ◦ c) Roland Barthes
    - ◦ d) Sigmund Freud
      Answer: a) Jacques Derrida

32. **What is the concept of "différance" in Derridean Deconstruction?**

    - ◦ a) The idea that all texts have fixed meanings
    - ◦ b) The understanding that meaning is always deferred and never fully fixed
    - ◦ c) The belief in absolute truth within literature
    - ◦ d) The concept of binary oppositions
      Answer: b) The understanding that meaning is always deferred and never fully fixed

33. **What does Post-Structuralism reject about language?**

    - ◦ a) The notion of stable, unchanging meanings
    - ◦ b) The importance of context in interpretation
    - ◦ c) The role of the reader in constructing meaning
    - ◦ d) The study of texts as part of cultural systems
      Answer: a) The notion of stable, unchanging meanings

34. **Which term is central to Michel Foucault's Post-Structuralist theory?**

    - ◦ a) Genealogy
    - ◦ b) Decoding
    - ◦ c) Archetypes
    - ◦ d) Class struggle
      Answer: a) Genealogy

35. **What is the aim of Deconstruction?**

    - ◦ a) To uncover hidden, universal meanings
    - ◦ b) To demonstrate the fluid and unstable nature of language
    - ◦ c) To emphasize the importance of cultural contexts
    - ◦ d) To establish a single correct interpretation
      Answer: b) To demonstrate the fluid and unstable nature of language

36. **Which concept is central to Sigmund Freud's analysis of literature?**

- ◦ a) The Oedipus complex
- ◦ b) The role of societal norms in shaping texts
- ◦ c) Binary oppositions
- ◦ d) Archetypes
  Answer: a) The Oedipus complex

37. **Jacques Lacan expanded Freud's ideas, focusing on which concept?**

- ◦ a) The mirror stage
- ◦ b) Class struggle
- ◦ c) Structural systems of meaning
- ◦ d) The death of the author
  Answer: a) The mirror stage

38. **What does Psychoanalytic Criticism focus on in literature?**

- ◦ a) The moral lessons of the text
- ◦ b) The unconscious desires and motivations of characters
- ◦ c) The historical and cultural context
- ◦ d) The formal elements of writing
  Answer: b) The unconscious desires and motivations of characters

39. **According to Psychoanalytic criticism, what role does the unconscious mind play in literature?**

- ◦ a) It shapes the characters' external actions and desires
- ◦ b) It has no significant influence
- ◦ c) It helps structure the narrative
- ◦ d) It only relates to the reader's emotions
  Answer: a) It shapes the characters' external actions and desires

40. **In Psychoanalytic Criticism, what does the "mirror stage" refer to?**

- ◦ a) The moment when a character realizes their purpose in the narrative
- ◦ b) The phase where an individual forms their identity through reflection
- ◦ c) The reflection of societal ideals in the character
- ◦ d) The relationship between author and audience
  Answer: b) The phase where an individual forms their identity through reflection

41. **Which theorist is most associated with Marxist literary criticism?**

- ◦ a) Terry Eagleton
- ◦ b) Sigmund Freud
- ◦ c) Roland Barthes
- ◦ d) Jacques Derrida
  Answer: a) Terry Eagleton

42. **What is the central concern of Marxist Criticism?**

- ◦ a) The psychological state of characters
- ◦ b) The socioeconomic context and power structures in literature
- ◦ c) The form and structure of the text
- ◦ d) The representation of gender
  Answer: b) The socioeconomic context and power structures in literature

43. **Marxist Criticism explores how literature reflects which of the following?**

- ◦ a) The importance of aesthetics
- ◦ b) The material conditions of society
- ◦ c) The role of the individual
- ◦ d) The unconscious mind
  Answer: b) The material conditions of society

44. **Which of the following is an idea associated with Marxist literary criticism?**

- ◦ a) Literature reflects the values of the dominant class
- ◦ b) Literature is a product of individual imagination
- ◦ c) Literature can only be understood through formal analysis
- ◦ d) Literature should be evaluated based on artistic merit alone
  Answer: a) Literature reflects the values of the dominant class

45. **Who is considered the father of modern Marxist literary theory?**

- ◦ a) Sigmund Freud
- ◦ b) Karl Marx
- ◦ c) Terry Eagleton
- ◦ d) Roland Barthes
  Answer: b) Karl Marx

46. **Who is considered the father of modern Marxist literary theory?**

- ◦ a) Sigmund Freud
- ◦ b) Karl Marx
- ◦ c) Terry Eagleton
- ◦ d) Roland Barthes
  Answer: b) Karl Marx

47. **Which of the following best describes Feminist Criticism?**

- ◦ a) Analyzing literature in the context of historical events
- ◦ b) Analyzing the representation of gender and power dynamics
- ◦ c) Focusing on the form and structure of a text
- ◦ d) Studying the unconscious desires of characters
  Answer: b) Analyzing the representation of gender and power dynamics

48. **Which key feminist thinker argued that "one is not born, but rather becomes a woman"?**

- ◦ a) Simone de Beauvoir
- ◦ b) Judith Butler
- ◦ c) Elaine Showalter
- ◦ d) Julia Kristeva
  Answer: a) Simone de Beauvoir

49. **Judith Butler's concept of "gender performativity" suggests that:**

- ◦ a) Gender is an innate characteristic
- ◦ b) Gender identity is shaped by biological factors
- ◦ c) Gender is an ongoing performance shaped by societal norms
- ◦ d) Gender is unrelated to literary expression
  Answer: c) Gender is an ongoing performance shaped by societal norms

50. **Which of the following is a major focus of Feminist Criticism?**

- ◦ a) How literature reflects the concerns of male authors
- ◦ b) How gender dynamics shape literature and its interpretation
- ◦ c) The unconscious desires of female characters
- ◦ d) The aesthetic qualities of female authors' works
  Answer: b) How gender dynamics shape literature and its interpretation

51. **Which concept is central to Elaine Showalter's feminist theory?**

- ◦ a) The role of the female writer in creating literature
- ◦ b) The male gaze in literature
- ◦ c) The importance of female sexuality in texts
- ◦ d) The relationship between gender and class
  Answer: a) The role of the female writer in creating literature

52. **Postcolonial theory primarily focuses on the impact of:**

- ◦ a) Economic systems on literature
- ◦ b) Colonialism on culture and literature
- ◦ c) Feminist thought in the literary world
- ◦ d) The emotional states of characters
  Answer: b) Colonialism on culture and literature

53. **Who is the author of "Orientalism," a foundational text in postcolonial criticism?**

- ◦ a) Homi K. Bhabha
- ◦ b) Gayatri Spivak
- ◦ c) Edward Said

- ◦ d) Frantz Fanon
  Answer: c) Edward Said

54. **Postcolonial critics argue that colonialism:**

- ◦ a) Has little effect on cultural production
- ◦ b) Is irrelevant to modern literature
- ◦ c) Shapes the identities of both colonizers and the colonized
- ◦ d) Should be ignored in literary analysis

Answer: c) Shapes the identities of both colonizers and the colonized

55. **What is the concept of "the subaltern" in postcolonial criticism?**

- ◦ a) The dominant class in colonial society
- ◦ b) The indigenous population and their perspectives
- ◦ c) The colonial powers and their influence on culture
- ◦ d) The economic systems that reinforce colonialism

Answer: b) The indigenous population and their perspectives

56. **Which postcolonial theorist introduced the concept of "hybridity"?**

- ◦ a) Gayatri Spivak
- ◦ b) Homi K. Bhabha
- ◦ c) Frantz Fanon
- ◦ d) Aijaz Ahmad

Answer: b) Homi K. Bhabha

57. **Which of the following is a key idea in Ecocriticism?**

- ◦ a) The relationship between humans and nature in literature
- ◦ b) The study of gender and power dynamics
- ◦ c) The analysis of economic power structures
- ◦ d) The focus on individual psychology in texts

Answer: a) The relationship between humans and nature in literature

58. **Which of the following would most likely be studied in Ecocriticism?**

- ◦ a) The portrayal of ecological crises in literature
- ◦ b) The representation of gender roles in novels
- ◦ c) The development of the plot structure
- ◦ d) The unconscious motivations of characters

Answer: a) The portrayal of ecological crises in literature

59. **Which writer is commonly associated with the field of Ecocriticism?**

- ◦ a) Margaret Atwood
- ◦ b) William Wordsworth
- ◦ c) Karl Marx
- ◦ d) Judith Butler

Answer: a) Margaret Atwood

60. **What is the main concern of Environmental Justice in Ecocriticism?**

- ◦ a) Analyzing the role of technology in literature
- ◦ b) Addressing how literature represents ecological destruction and its social implications
- ◦ c) Studying the economic impacts of environmental changes
- ◦ d) Focusing on the aesthetic quality of nature writing
  Answer: b) Addressing how literature represents ecological destruction and its social implications

61. **Which of the following is a key question in Ecocriticism?**

- ◦ a) How does literature reflect social power structures?

- ◦ b) How does literature represent the relationship between humans and the environment?
- ◦ c) What are the unconscious desires of the characters in a text?
- ◦ d) How do gender roles influence character development?
  Answer: b) How does literature represent the relationship between humans and the environment?

62. **Who is one of the leading figures in Ecocriticism and the study of nature in literature?**

- ◦ a) Ursula K. Le Guin
- ◦ b) Tim Morton
- ◦ c) George Orwell
- ◦ d) Terry Eagleton
  Answer: b) Tim Morton

63. **Which of the following describes the "ecological imagination"?**

- ◦ a) Imagining nature as an independent and separate entity from human experience
- ◦ b) The ability to consider ecological concerns in literature and how humans interact with the environment
- ◦ c) The desire to transform nature into a human-made construct
- ◦ d) A focus on human civilization's triumph over nature
  Answer: b) The ability to consider ecological concerns in literature and how humans interact with the environment

64. **Which literary form is particularly popular in Ecocriticism for exploring nature?**

- ◦ a) Tragedy
- ◦ b) Nature writing
- ◦ c) Epic poetry
- ◦ d) Satire
  Answer: b) Nature writing

65. **Which of the following is NOT a concern of Ecocriticism?**

- ◦ a) Environmental justice
- ◦ b) The representation of ecosystems in literature
- ◦ c) Binary oppositions between nature and culture
- ◦ d) Psychological development of individual characters
  Answer: d) Psychological development of individual characters

66. **Which literary theorist is known for emphasizing the importance of 'the social function of literature' in Marxist thought?**

  - ◦ a) Terry Eagleton
  - ◦ b) Roland Barthes
  - ◦ c) Sigmund Freud
  - ◦ d) Homi K. Bhabha
  - **Answer: a) Terry Eagleton**

67. **Which of the following is an argument made by Post-Structuralist critics?**

  - ◦ a) Texts have a fixed meaning that can be interpreted universally
  - ◦ b) Meaning in literature is determined by the reader and never fixed
  - ◦ c) The form of a text is the most important aspect of interpretation
  - ◦ d) The author's intention is the sole key to understanding a text
  - **Answer: b) Meaning in literature is determined by the reader and never fixed**

68. **What is the key concept in Jacques Derrida's Deconstruction?**

  - ◦ a) The importance of authorial intention
  - ◦ b) The analysis of binary oppositions and their instability
  - ◦ c) The moral message of literature
  - ◦ d) The importance of historical context
  - **Answer: b) The analysis of binary oppositions and their instability**

69. **In Marxist criticism, literature is seen as a reflection of:**

  - ◦ a) The unconscious mind
  - ◦ b) The economic base and class struggles
  - ◦ c) Personal emotions and individual experiences
  - ◦ d) The aesthetic and formal qualities of writing
  - **Answer: b) The economic base and class struggles**

70. **Who is the philosopher associated with the idea of "interpellation" in Marxist theory?**

  - ◦ a) Sigmund Freud
  - ◦ b) Louis Althusser
  - ◦ c) Roland Barthes
  - ◦ d) Michel Foucault
  - **Answer: b) Louis Althusser**

71. **Who is a prominent figure in the study of nature writing, a key genre for Ecocriticism?**

  - ◦ a) Henry David Thoreau
  - ◦ b) F. Scott Fitzgerald
  - ◦ c) Samuel Johnson
  - ◦ d) Karl Marx
  - **Answer: a) Henry David Thoreau**

72. **Feminist literary criticism examines:**

- a) The unconscious motivations of male characters
- b) The depiction of women and gender dynamics in literature
- c) The impact of historical events on literature
- d) The role of literary form and technique
  Answer: b) The depiction of women and gender dynamics in literature

73. **The idea of "literature as ideology" was introduced by:**

- a) Terry Eagleton
- b) Roland Barthes
- c) John Dryden
- d) Matthew Arnold
  Answer: a) Terry Eagleton

74. **Which theory focuses on the relationship between language and power?**

- a) Structuralism
- b) Deconstruction
- c) Postcolonial theory
- d) Feminist criticism
  Answer: c) Postcolonial theory

75. **Which of the following is NOT a focus of Structuralism?**

- a) Language as a system of signs
- b) Binary oppositions within texts
- c) The role of the unconscious in character development

- d) How texts communicate underlying meanings
  Answer: c) The role of the unconscious in character development

76. **The "mirror stage" in Lacanian Psychoanalysis refers to:**

- a) A moment in a character's narrative development
- b) A period of individual identity formation
- c) The reflection of societal values in texts
- d) The role of the author's intention
  Answer: b) A period of individual identity formation

77. **Ecocriticism has been increasingly concerned with:**

- a) The role of technological advances in literature
- b) The impact of ecological crises on humanity and nature
- c) The study of the historical context of literary works
- d) The unconscious desires in nature-related texts
  Answer: b) The impact of ecological crises on humanity and nature

78. **In Post-Structuralism, meaning is:**

  - ◦ a) Stable and fixed
  - ◦ b) Constructed through the reader's interpretation
  - ◦ c) Determined by the author's intention
  - ◦ d) Based on formal aspects of the text
    Answer: b) Constructed through the reader's interpretation

79. **Which of the following is a major tenet of Feminist Criticism?**

  - ◦ a) The study of female sexuality in literature
  - ◦ b) The rejection of gender as a concept in literature
  - ◦ c) The idea that literary form determines meaning
  - ◦ d) A focus on historical events in literary production
    Answer: a) The study of female sexuality in literature

80. **Which of the following is a common focus of Ecocriticism?**

  - ◦ a) The analysis of the human-nature relationship in texts
  - ◦ b) The historical context of texts
  - ◦ c) The analysis of class struggles in literature
  - ◦ d) The focus on individual character psychology
    Answer: a) The analysis of the human-nature relationship in texts

81. **Which of the following thinkers is known for his concept of "archetypes" in literature?**

  - ◦ a) Sigmund Freud
  - ◦ b) Carl Jung
  - ◦ c) Roland Barthes
  - ◦ d) Terry Eagleton
    Answer: b) Carl Jung

82. **Which of the following approaches is most likely to examine the power relations embedded in texts?**

  - ◦ a) Structuralism
  - ◦ b) Feminist criticism
  - ◦ c) Ecocriticism
  - ◦ d) Formalism
    Answer: b) Feminist criticism

83. **Which theory emerged as a reaction against the ideas of Structuralism?**

  - ◦ a) Formalism

  - ◦ b) Marxism
  - ◦ c) Post-Structuralism
  - ◦ d) Psychoanalysis
    Answer: c) Post-Structuralism

84. **Which of the following is central to Ecofeminism within Ecocriticism?**

- ◦ a) The critique of gender inequality in literary representations of nature
- ◦ b) The study of environmental degradation in literature
- ◦ c) The analysis of socio-economic class in literature
- ◦ d) The examination of historical contexts in nature writing
  Answer: a) The critique of gender inequality in literary representations of nature

85. **Who is associated with the concept of "the death of the author"?**

- ◦ a) Roland Barthes
- ◦ b) Jacques Derrida
- ◦ c) Michel Foucault
- ◦ d) Terry Eagleton
  Answer: a) Roland Barthes

86. **Which literary approach examines how texts represent ideologies and power structures?**

- ◦ a) Psychoanalytic Criticism
- ◦ b) Feminist Criticism
- ◦ c) Marxist Criticism
- ◦ d) Ecocriticism
  Answer: c) Marxist Criticism

87. **Who is the author of *Poetics*, a foundational text in classical literary theory?**

- ◦ a) Horace
- ◦ b) Plato
- ◦ c) Aristotle
- ◦ d) Longinus
  Answer: c) Aristotle

88. **What is the concept of *mimesis* in classical literary theory?**

- ◦ a) The imitation of human emotion
- ◦ b) The representation of reality in art
- ◦ c) The catharsis experienced by the audience
- ◦ d) The unifying theme of a work
  Answer: b) The representation of reality in art

89. **Which philosopher emphasized the idea of catharsis in tragedy?**

- ◦ a) Plato
- ◦ b) Aristotle
- ◦ c) Horace
- ◦ d) John Dryden
  Answer: b) Aristotle

90. In Neoclassical literary theory, what is the principle of *decorum*?

- ◦ a) The use of supernatural elements
- ◦ b) The adherence to proper behavior and language for characters
- ◦ c) The exploration of the inner psyche of characters
- ◦ d) The avoidance of moral instruction in literature
  Answer: b) The adherence to proper behavior and language for characters

91. Which Neoclassical thinker wrote *Ars Poetica*, focusing on rules for writing poetry?

- ◦ a) Horace
- ◦ b) Longinus
- ◦ c) John Dryden
- ◦ d) Samuel Johnson
  Answer: a) Horace

92. What concept did William Wordsworth champion in Romantic literary theory?

- ◦ a) The importance of emotion and imagination in poetry
- ◦ b) The supremacy of reason over emotion
- ◦ c) The role of art as a social commentary
- ◦ d) The imitation of classical models in literature
  Answer: a) The importance of emotion and imagination in poetry

93. Who is a key critic associated with the Victorian theory of *art for art's sake*?

- ◦ a) John Ruskin
- ◦ b) Matthew Arnold
- ◦ c) Walter Pater
- ◦ d) Percy Bysshe Shelley
  Answer: c) Walter Pater

94. Which of the following is a primary concern of Formalism in literary theory?

- ◦ a) Authorial intent
- ◦ b) The structure and language of the text itself
- ◦ c) Historical context of the text
- ◦ d) Social and economic influences on literature
  Answer: b) The structure and language of the text itself

95. Which structuralist theorist is known for his work on signs and the theory of the signifier/signified?

- ◦ a) Jacques Derrida
- ◦ b) Roland Barthes
- ◦ c) Ferdinand de Saussure

- ◦ d) Michel Foucault
  Answer: c) Ferdinand de Saussure

96. What concept is central to Jacques Derrida's Deconstruction theory?

- a) The unconscious mind
- b) Binary oppositions and their instability
- c) The historical background of texts
- d) The economic implications of literature

Answer: b) Binary oppositions and their instability

97. Who expanded Freudian psychoanalysis in literary theory and focused on the *mirror stage*?

- a) Sigmund Freud
- b) Jacques Lacan
- c) Carl Jung
- d) Julia Kristeva

Answer: b) Jacques Lacan

98. What concept is central to Marxist criticism in literature?

- a) The role of the author's intention in shaping meaning
- b) The focus on the economic and social context of literature
- c) The unconscious desires of characters
- d) The role of the sublime in shaping texts

Answer: b) The focus on the economic and social context of literature

99. Which feminist critic argued that "one is not born, but rather becomes a woman"?

- a) Elaine Showalter
- b) Simone de Beauvoir
- c) Judith Butler
- d) Kate Millett

Answer: b) Simone de Beauvoir

100. Which of the following is a major theme in Postcolonial criticism?

- a) The subconscious motives of characters
- b) The impact of colonialism on culture and identity
- c) The structure of the narrative
- d) The moral lessons in literature

Answer: b) The impact of colonialism on culture and identity

BIBILIOGRAPHY

Aristotle. *Poetics*. Translated by S. H. Butcher, Dover Publications, 1997.

Arnold, Matthew. *Culture and Anarchy*. Edited by J. Dover Wilson, Cambridge University Press, 1960.

Barthes, Roland. *Image-Music-Text*. Translated by Stephen Heath, Hill and Wang, 1977.

Bhabha, Homi K. *The Location of Culture*. Routledge, 1994.

Brooks, Cleanth. *The Well Wrought Urn: Studies in the Structure of Poetry*. Harcourt, 1947.

Coleridge, Samuel Taylor. *Biographia Literaria*. Edited by George Watson, Everyman's Library, 1990.

Derrida, Jacques. *Of Grammatology*. Translated by Gayatri Chakravorty Spivak, Johns Hopkins University Press, 1976.

Dryden, John. *An Essay of Dramatic Poesy*. Oxford University Press, 2004.

Foucault, Michel. *The Archaeology of Knowledge*. Translated by A. M. Sheridan Smith, Routledge, 2002.

Freud, Sigmund. *The Interpretation of Dreams*. Translated by James Strachey, Basic Books, 2010.

Longinus. *On the Sublime*. Translated by W. H. Fyfe, Harvard University Press, 1995.

Pater, Walter. *The Renaissance: Studies in Art and Poetry*. Oxford University Press, 1998.

Said, Edward W. *Orientalism*. Vintage Books, 1979.

Saussure, Ferdinand de. *Course in General Linguistics*. Edited by Charles Bally and Albert Sechehaye, translated by Wade Baskin, McGraw-Hill, 1966.

Showalter, Elaine. *A Literature of Their Own: British Women Novelists from Brontë to Lessing*. Princeton University Press, 1977.

Shelley, Percy Bysshe. *A Defence of Poetry and Other Essays*. Prometheus Books, 2004.

Spivak, Gayatri Chakravorty. "Can the Subaltern Speak?" *Colonial Discourse and Post-Colonial Theory: A Reader*, edited by Patrick Williams and Laura Chrisman, Columbia University Press, 1994, pp. 66–111.

Wordsworth, William. *Preface to Lyrical Ballads*. Oxford World's Classics, Oxford University Press, 2000.